MILES·LEWIS

KING OF THE ICE

MILES·LEWIS
⚡ KING OF THE ICE ⚡

by Kelly Starling Lyons
illustrated by Wayne Spencer

Penguin Workshop

W

PENGUIN WORKSHOP
An imprint of Penguin Random House LLC, New York

First published in the United States of America by Penguin Workshop,
an imprint of Penguin Random House LLC, New York, 2022

Visit us online at penguinrandomhouse.com.

Library of Congress Cataloging-in-Publication Data is available.

Manufactured in China

ISBN 9780593383490 (paperback)   10 9 8 7 6 5 4 3 2 1 TOPL
ISBN 9780593383506 (library binding)   10 9 8 7 6 5 4 3 2 1 TOPL

For my brother Kevin, who cheered for my new series and encouraged me to explore Black history in hockey—KSL

For Dommie, Ali, and Josephine, who teach me something new every day; and to my mom, who encouraged me well past the point of reason—WS

CHAPTER ONE

Game On

Skating is serious business in my family. My mom and dad can glide backward, spin in circles, bop to the music. They said the roller rink was the place to be when they were growing up. They love to tell people they met at a spot called Spinning Wheels back in their hometown of Pittsburgh. I know. Kinda corny, but it makes me smile.

Me? I like skating okay. But bike riding, that's my thing. Coasting down a hill with the wind in my face, pumping my legs as I jet down a trail—I'm with that any day. That's why I sighed at first when

my teacher, Miss Taylor, said that
our next field trip was going to the
rink.

My boy RJ caught me.

"What's wrong, Miles?" he
whispered.

"Nothing," I said. "I just hoped we were going someplace different."

All around me on the orange-and-blue carpet, my friends cheesed. Jada, Lena, and Simone nudged one another. Carson whispered to Gabi. Soon, our class rumbled with energy like a crowd getting hyped before a big game.

Fourth grade already had more field trips than third. I guess skating wasn't so bad.

"Class, class," Miss Taylor said to settle everyone down.

"Yes, yes," we answered.

"I know you're excited. Let's go over the details. We're not going to just any skating rink. We're going *ice*-skating. Did you know that skating can teach you a lot about physics?"

Did Miss Taylor say physics? I sat up straight. Now we were talking. If there was something I liked as much as riding bikes, it was science and technology. Rock collecting, doing experiments with my chemistry set, building robots, and flying drones. Maybe this field trip would be better than I thought.

"Has anyone gone ice-skating before?" Miss Taylor asked.

"Gabi and I are on hockey teams," Carson said.

My friend Jada raised her hand.

"I went ice-skating with my

cousins when we were visiting
family in New York City," she said.
"I fell a few times, but I got it by the
end."

Lena took ice-skating lessons.
RJ had gone before, too. I wondered

why I'd never tried it. As my friends shared what it was like, it sounded kinda tricky. But I could roller-skate and was pretty good at picking up new things. I wasn't sweating it. How hard could it be?

At recess, RJ and I headed for kickball with Gabi and Kyla. The girls had their own conversation going. RJ put his hand on my shoulder.

"Miles, you got me beat in most sports," he said. "I'm so glad I have one up on you."

"What are you talking about? It's not a competition."

"I'm talking about ice-skating," he said. "Finally, *finally*, I know how to do something you haven't tried."

I shrugged. If that made him feel good, cool.

"You're *definitely* gonna wipe out at least once," he said.

Made sense that I might fall as I learned, but the way he said it made me roll my eyes.

"Don't worry, I'll be there to help you up."

Gabi and Kyla grew quiet like our conversation just got interesting. I didn't know why RJ was making a big deal out of this, but I wasn't going to let him talk trash.

"It may be my first time, but I don't know if I'll be falling. I can skate."

"You sure about that?" he said. "How about a bet?"

Bet? It was like that word echoed through the playground and caught everyone's attention. Bet. Bet. Bet. I heard whispering and felt stares on my back.

"If you skate without falling, I'll put a 'Miles is the man' sign on my backpack. If you fall, you have to put one on yours saying that I am."

RJ was my friend, but he loved competition. Too much sometimes. This whole thing was silly—I just wanted to learn about physics and have some fun. But now that everybody was listening, I was on the spot.

"Bet," I agreed.

The pressure was on.

CHAPTER TWO

Looking Like Me

When the school bus pulled up to my stop, I bumped fists with RJ and hopped off. I could see Nana down the block weeding in the front of our house. She wiped her glistening face with her arm and smiled when she spotted me. The silver in her locs shone in the sunlight.

"There's my boy," she said when

I bent down and kissed her cheek. "How was your day?"

"It was pretty good," I said. "I aced a test and found out we're going on an ice-skating field trip."

"Sounds fun," she said. "I did some skating in my day."

"*Ice*-skating?"

"Yes, sir. Don't sound so shocked. Your nana knows a few things," she said, winking. "Got a lot of homework?"

"Already did it. I'll take my backpack in and come out and help."

I don't know why I was surprised that Nana could ice-skate. Just when I thought I knew everything about her, she revealed something else.

Like the time she pointed herself out as an extra in a movie we were watching. Or when she told us about the time she had filled in for a famous singer when his bus didn't make it to the club on time.

Inside, her paintings gave clues about her life. A brown girl standing behind a microphone onstage. People of all ages protesting with picket signs raised high. A picture of my granddad, who passed away when I was little, in an air force uniform. A portrait of our family—Momma, Dad, Nana, and me—holding hands around the dinner table. That was my favorite.

Sometimes I wished there was

another kid in the picture with us. Don't get me wrong—being an only child had perks. No fights over what to watch on TV or what video games to play. No battling for attention. But some days, I missed having someone my age to hang with, celebrate holidays, and share secrets. I guess that's why I loved being around my friends so much.

I ran upstairs to my room, dropped off my backpack, and changed into an old T-shirt and sweats. I grabbed some garden gloves and headed outside.

"I thought you got lost," Nana said without looking up. I could hear the smile in her voice.

I kneeled next to her in the dirt and got busy. I had to use both hands to pull out a stubborn patch of leafy plants. The roots ran deep.

"Tell me about ice-skating," I said.

"That was a long time ago, honey. Feels like another life. On TV, I never saw ice-skaters who looked like us with Olympic medals. I set it in my mind that I would change that. I practiced and got pretty good, but there was a lot I wanted to do. Art and music ended up calling to me more."

I hadn't thought about ice-skating being something that could make a difference. That was cool. For a minute, I thought about telling Nana about RJ's bet. But I knew what she would say. Her voice rang out in my head: *We taught you better than to follow along with something you don't feel good about. You should have set him straight.*

Nana and I worked side by side until the weeds were out of the ground and in the lawn bag.

"We can mulch next week," she said, dusting off her pants as she stood. "Now it's time to get washed up. We smell like outside." I headed upstairs to take a shower and change my clothes. My parents were on their way home with dinner. Fridays were our eating-out days. They both worked at the university, so sometimes they drove to work together.

I came down just as they were coming in.

"Hey, Miles," Momma said, giving me a hug. Dad pulled me into one, too, after setting the bags of food on the table. The savory smell made my stomach grumble. I read the name of

the restaurant on the bags: Catch of
the Sea. Looked like we were having
fish tonight.

I washed my hands and set the
dining room table so we could all eat
together. Nana blessed the food, and
we dug in.

"Anything new at school?" Momma asked.

"Nothing much," I said. "We're going ice-skating for a field trip next week."

"Ice-skating, huh?" Dad said. "Maybe you'll get into it and want to try hockey like my man Willie O'Ree."

"Who's that?"

Uh-oh. Why did I say that? Dad was a Black history professor and was famous for his homework assignments.

"Sounds like you need to hit the books, son," he said. "You know I don't just give out answers. That's too easy."

"Look it up on the computer after dinner," Momma said. She was a techie. "Let us know what you find out."

Why couldn't Dad just tell me? Now, I had to wait to find out who Willie O'Ree was. As soon as I finished eating, I put my plate in the sink and headed for the stairs.

"Aren't you forgetting something,

Miles?" Momma said.

She glanced at the table.

Right. I had to help clean up. When I was done, I made a beeline for my room to look up Willie O'Ree online. His picture came up first. He reminded me a little of Nana's

brother, my uncle Ray. I clicked on one of the articles. Willie O'Ree was the first Black hockey player in the National Hockey League. They called him the "Jackie Robinson" of ice hockey, because they both broke racial barriers. Over his career in the minor leagues and NHL, he dealt with name-calling, racist taunts, people doing horrible things like spitting at him, throwing drinks at him, and starting fights with him, but he never gave up. I nodded and wrote his name in the notebook I fill with facts about important events and people. Willie O'Ree. That was someone I would remember.

Before getting up, I heard a ding.

It was an invite from RJ, Jada, and Gabi to play a video game. Before joining them, I saw I had a private message from RJ, too.

"Hope you're getting my sign ready," it said.

I sighed. He never let up. Somebody needed to teach RJ a lesson. Maybe it would be me.

CHAPTER THREE

Secret Weapon

ield trip day would be here before I knew it. I lived in a house of skaters—that gave me an edge. Nana taking me ice-skating would be cheating. But there was nothing wrong with her giving me tips.

"Nana, do you think you could give me some ice-skating pointers?" I asked Saturday morning.

"Sure, honey," she said, "when
I get back. I'm running late for an
appointment. We can talk skating all
you want later today."

She rushed out the door and didn't say where she was going. That was kinda weird, but I didn't want to be nosy and ask.

I got some orange juice and  noticed a flyer on the kitchen table. I saw the words "luxury apartments and town-homes for independent seniors." My stomach dropped.

What was that for? Was Nana thinking about moving? I held the paper in my hand, frozen in my spot.

No way. She couldn't leave. It hurt to even think about her not being here. I put the flyer back on the table and turned it over as if that would make it disappear.

My thoughts raced as I trudged upstairs to my room. Was Nana unhappy living with us? Did I take up too much of her time? Why did she want a place by herself? Each step felt like I was moving through mud. I flopped on my bed and tried to think about something else.

"Hey, Miles," Momma said, sticking her head in my room after a while. "Start wrapping up whatever you're doing. Don't forget you're getting together with RJ in a few."

The basketball hang out. I sighed. I did forget. I really wasn't in the mood to see him. But I got up and started getting ready.

When Momma and I got to the park near our school, Brookside Elementary, RJ and his mom were already there shooting hoops.

"I'll let you take over," Miss Nikki said.

She hugged my mom. They sat on a nearby bench and started talking.

"Horse?" RJ asked, dribbling the ball.

He had on his favorite blue Air Jordan hoodie, the one he wore when he was serious about playing.

I nodded. This was our game. You

had to copy the other person's shot. If you missed it, you got an *H*. The next one you missed, you got an *O*. If you spelled out all the letters of *horse*, you lost.

"You can go first," I said.

RJ made a layup. That meant I had to make the same shot. *Swish.* It sailed in.

"That was just a warm-up," RJ said, dribbling the ball while he eyed me. "Let's see if you can do this."

Jump shot, hook shot, over his shoulder, behind the hoop. He sank some and missed some. Each time I was up, he looked like he was holding his breath, hoping that my shots wouldn't make it in. But I was lucky. I matched his flow, missing a few and nailing others.

Finally, we both had *H-O-R-S.*

RJ knew this could be it. He dribbled the ball way out to three-point land. He knew that was my weakest shot. A long look at me and then he lifted the ball in his hands, focused on the hoop, and let it fly. It circled the rim and . . . landed on the ground.

He winced.

"That was so close," I said.

He didn't say anything, just nodded and twisted his lips.

"You're up."

I didn't know if I would make it, but I knew how RJ was. I thought about missing it on purpose. That way, no one would win. But I remembered how it felt when RJ was being so competitive. I was tired of it.

I took a breath and focused on my goal. Hand arched. Ball raised in the air. I let it go and felt like it was moving in slow motion. I saw RJ's eyes following the ball, too. *Swoosh.* Nothing but net.

RJ came over to me with his hand raised to give me some love.

"I can't hate, Miles," RJ said, giving me a pound. "That was a nasty shot. But we still got our bet. Let's see how you do with that."

What RJ said didn't even bother me. I had bigger things on my mind. As Momma and I drove home, I kept thinking about that paper I saw.

"You okay, Miles?"

"I'm fine," I said. "Just thinking about something I need to figure out."

"Want some help?"

"No, I got it," I said.

"I know you do, but I'm here if you need me."

Nana was in her room when we got home.

"How was your appointment?" I asked, standing in the doorway.

"It was good. Really good. Now, I promised you some skating talk. Come on in and have a seat."

But I didn't want to hear about skating anymore. I wanted to know where she went and why. I tried to listen to her tips but heard a voice inside asking questions instead. Did Nana really want to move? She had been living with us since I was in kindergarten. Hard to remember when she wasn't here. What would it take for her to stay?

CHAPTER FOUR

The Science of Skating

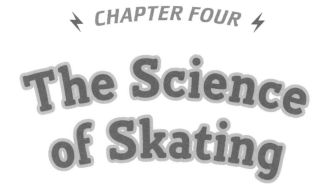

Monday morning, Miss Taylor started our lesson on physics to get us ready for the trip.

"How many of you have slipped on ice?"

I raised my hand, along with a few others. I still remembered how my backside ached when it hit the driveway.

"Think of how hard it is to have control. What helps skaters start and stop on the ice?"

She wrote a word on the whiteboard in big purple letters: friction.

"When you're skating and gliding, there's little friction between the skates and the ice. But when it's time to push off or stop, the blades of the skates can cut into the ice and can give you the traction you need."

Next, she reviewed Newton's first law of motion.

"Anyone remember what it is?"

Jada raised her hand. "An object at rest stays at rest, and an object in motion stays in motion."

"How does that relate to skating?"

I tried to focus, but I kept thinking about Nana and that silly bet with RJ. Even learning about science couldn't get me out of my funk.

Miss Taylor caught me staring into space.

"What do you think, Miles?"

"Uh, I'm not sure," I said. Then, I fessed up.

"Sorry, Miss Taylor. I wasn't paying attention."

"Thanks for being honest, Miles," she said. "But I need you to be here."

The rest of the lesson, I took notes, but I still felt like I was two steps behind. Miss Taylor talked about different kinds of skates—ones with four wheels, in-line, and ice skates—and how they were different and similar.

"You okay, Miles?" Jada asked as we lined up for lunch. She knew if I missed a science question, I was out of it.

"Yeah," I said, and wished it were true.

As I ate my chicken nuggets, I

tried to think of how to convince
Nana to stay. I could tell her how
much I'd miss her. Or even better,
what if I showed her how much
she meant to us and how much we
needed her? Then she would never
want to leave.

When we hit the playground after
lunch, Jada came over.

"I heard about your bet with RJ,"

she said. "Why are you doing that?"

"I don't know," I said. "RJ tried to trash talk me. Before I knew it, I was in."

"You shouldn't do it if you don't want to," she said. "Forget about the bet. Just have fun."

"Jada, you coming?" Simone called her over to double Dutch with her, Carson, and Lena.

"See you, Miles."

Jada was right. I thought about what she said as I joined Gabi, RJ, Kyla, and the crew for kickball. Maybe I should just call the bet off.

But on the bus ride home, RJ kept trying to get under my skin.

"I want the sign in my favorite

color, green," he said. "Make the letters real big so everyone can see."

"Whatever, RJ," I said.

"Why you mad?" he said. "You can't be good at everything."

I was worried about Nana, and RJ was getting on my nerves.

"I didn't say I was," I snapped back. "Why are you being a hater?"

RJ crinkled his eyebrows and had a strange expression, like he couldn't believe I said that. He turned to the window. We rode the rest of the way without talking. I got out a book and pretended to read. When we got to my stop, I couldn't wait to get off. Nana wasn't outside when I walked up. I found her in the living room packing up things in boxes. My stomach dropped again.

"What are those for?" I asked.

"Just passing on some things I don't need."

This was getting serious. Time to put my plan into action.

"Nana, could you help me with homework?"

"Sure, I can try."

We sat at the dining room table and went over my vocabulary lesson together. She quizzed me on the words.

"Looks like you know these pretty well," she said. "I'm impressed."

"Thanks, Nana," I said. "That's

because you helped make it stick. What would I do without you?"

"I think you'd do okay," she said, winking. "You got a good head, Miles. That's all you need."

Why did she say that? I needed her, too. This wasn't going the way I wanted.

"Nana, can I ride my bike around the loop? I'll change clothes first."

"Sure, honey."

Whenever I'm riding, it's like all my worries fly away and my mind is as free as the wind. In the garage, I buckled my helmet and hopped on my bike. Before I knew it, I wasn't thinking about Nana or RJ. I just focused on pedaling. It felt good as

my legs pumped and took me down
our street to the cul-de-sac, around
the loop and back. Again and again.

I smiled and waved at Nana
when I saw her working in her herb
garden. I parked my bike and got

an idea. When Momma and Dad got home, I asked if we could go to the store to buy some mulch.

"Did Nana want us to pick it up?"

"No, I want to surprise her and do it myself."

"That's so thoughtful, Miles," Momma said. "She'll love it."

"So what made you think of surprising Nana?" Dad asked on the way there.

"She does a lot. I wanted to do something for her."

"That's right, Miles," he said with pride in his voice. "Mom is always there for us. You're growing up. Now, tell me, what did you learn about Willie O'Ree?"

I laughed. It might be a few days later, but Dad always remembered to follow up.

"He was amazing," I said. "It must have been so hard dealing with people calling him names while he played hockey just because of the color of his skin. But he kept going."

"Yeah, he paved the way. There was a Colored Hockey League in Canada before Willie O'Ree's time. There's even a postage stamp honoring them."

"Like the Negro leagues of baseball here? That's cool."

Learning about hockey history made ice-skating feel more important, like I was going to be part of a legacy. Nana made me feel like that, too. Gardening with her, painting, and staying up to watch old movies—that was something special I didn't want to end.

When we got back, I got busy. I
spread the reddish-brown mulch
around the bushes and the tree
in the front yard, making sure it
looked neat and even. I stood in the
driveway and smiled at my work. It
looked good—Nana had taught me
well. I couldn't wait until she saw it.

I raced inside and told her I had
something to show her.

"Excuse me a minute," she said to the person she was speaking to on the phone, using her business voice.

"You see me talking, Miles. I'll be off soon."

Ouch. I just wanted her to see the surprise. I kept walking through the room. Seemed like she was never getting off the call. I wondered who she was talking to. I caught a few words: "It looked real nice. How soon will it be ready?" Was the call about a new place to live? My heart raced. I didn't even want to think about it. Finally, Nana hung up.

"Okay, Miles, what was so important that you forgot your manners?"

"Sorry, Nana," I said, grabbing her hand and tugging gently. "But there's something you have to check out."

"I'm coming," she said, laughing. "I'm coming."

When she walked outside, her face said it all. She beamed at the

neat spread of mulch.

"You did this?" she said, looking at me. "All by yourself?"

I smiled and nodded.

"I'm so proud of you. Looks like I can hang up my gardening gloves. The torch has been passed."

Hang up her gloves? No. That wasn't the plan. This was going all wrong. I wanted Nana to see how much we appreciated her, not that I could do it without her.

No brother or sister was bad enough. But I always told myself that at least I had Momma, Dad, and Nana. That was something special. Now, she might be moving. What was I going to do?

I felt that drop in my stomach again. Things just weren't working out.

CHAPTER FIVE

Balancing Act

O n field trip day, a chill ran through me before I even got to the rink. I sat next to Carson on the way there.

RJ sat next to Kyla and kept turning to look at me. I knew the bet didn't really matter, but it felt like everything was out of control. I needed something to go my way.

Inside, we lined up to get our skates. I found a spot to put mine on and saw RJ on his way to where I was. I tried not to look at him.

"You might get lucky and not fall," he said, pulling on his skates and tying the laces. "But if you do, remember our bet."

I didn't answer. Remember? How could I forget? RJ wouldn't let me. The instructors checked that our skates were on securely so we had support around our ankles. Next, it was time to stand up. I felt weird balancing on the blade. The instructors covered some rules, teaching us how to stop, keep our balance, and fall safely. It was time to follow them to the rink.

Though it was warm outside, we had on sweaters, jackets, and gloves so we wouldn't be too cold in the indoor rink. I still shivered as I stepped onto the slippery floor.

I marched like they told us to as I got used to the feel of the skates on the ice. I thought knowing how to roller skate would help, but this felt completely different. Maybe RJ would win the bet after all.

We learned how to push off and glide. That wasn't too bad. We played some games, too, skating over to pick up a bean bag and make our way back. When it was my turn, I tried to keep my feet together with a little space between them, but I could feel them spreading farther and farther apart. I did what the instructors said not to do: Waved my arms to try to steady myself. I almost lost it. Then, I remembered the tip about touching my knees. Whew—close one. I saw RJ watching me.

"Good job, Miles," the instructor said.

We came off the ice and sat at tables while Miss Taylor talked about figure skating and kinetic energy. Then we got some time to try skating on our own. I saw Jada and Lena encouraging Simone as she wobbled along the edge of the rink.

She looked like a fawn learning to walk. Is that how I looked, too?

I stayed close to the wall in case I needed support. RJ skated next to me.

"How's it going?" he said. "Tougher than it looks, right? Need some help?"

I didn't know if he was serious or trying to be funny.

"I got it."

"Whatever."

He skated off and left me creeping along the rink. I was focusing so hard on not falling that I wasn't having fun at all.

As I watched my friends laughing and skating together, I decided to stop playing it safe. I pushed off and glided just as RJ was skating past.

"Watch it," he warned.

But it was too late. We crashed into each other, and I felt my legs give out. Before I knew it, we were both on our bottoms.

"You did that on purpose," he said.

"Come on, RJ," I said. "I fell on purpose. Why would I do that? Why are you acting this way?"

"I'm just tired of you always being the best in everything," he said. "I just wanted to have something. Now everyone saw me fall. You took that, too."

He didn't look at me and sounded upset. I didn't know he felt like that. That was messed up. There were plenty of things he did better than me.

"Did you forget that you always smash me when we play *Roblox*?" I said. "You play piano—I can't do that. You run faster than me. You hit three-pointers more than me. But we shouldn't be competing, we're friends."

"Yeah," he said. "I guess sitting out here on the ice, neither one of us is the man."

We looked at each other and laughed.

"Why don't we just have fun?" I said. "But first, can you help me get up?"

RJ grinned.

"Bet."

CHAPTER SIX

Ice Dreams

After the big fall, I stopped worrying about trying to impress and started to get the hang of skating on ice. I thought about Willie O'Ree and the Colored Hockey League in Canada and held my head high as I glided around the rink. Skating felt good. Nana would be proud.

Nana. What was I going to do? She

always said to deal with problems head-on. Enough worrying—we needed to talk.

★

When I got home and opened the door, I smelled vanilla and butter. I knew what that was.

"You made pound cake," I said, smiling at Nana.

"Just took it out a few minutes ago," she said. "Want a slice?"

No way was I turning that down. I put down my backpack and followed her into the kitchen.

I saw the golden brown cake on a crystal stand on the island. I walked over to get a closer look and spotted something else, too: a furniture store booklet. My mouth hung open. I couldn't believe it. Right where everyone could see! Suddenly, I wasn't hungry anymore. Before I could stop it, the words were out.

"Why didn't you tell me you were moving?"

There. I'd asked the question that made my head pound and my stomach turn flips.

"Moving? Where did you hear that?"

Nana usually told it to me straight. It wasn't like her to answer a question with a question. Something was up.

"I saw the paper about the senior apartments and town-homes."

She gave me one of those you-know-you're-out-of-line stares.

"Miles DuBois Lewis, what were you doing going through my things?"

I looked down.

"No, ma'am, I wasn't. I didn't. I found it on the table."

"Mmm-hmm. And you thought it was for me? Why didn't you just ask?"

I guess I didn't really want to hear what her answer would be.

 Suddenly, my throat got thick. I couldn't talk. I sniffed and tried to hold it in, but everything blurred, and a tear rolled down my cheek.

I wiped it away with the back of my hand.

"Aw, honey," she said, coming over and giving me a hug. "I'm sorry you were so worried. You know I wouldn't look into leaving without letting you know. A friend of mine is searching for a place. I was helping her find a good one."

"It wasn't for you?"

"I might move one day," she said.

My stomach fluttered.

"It's nice to have your own space sometimes. But no time soon. You're stuck with me."

I hugged her close. I hoped she wouldn't leave for a long time. I filled her in on how much fun I had

ice-skating. She had a great idea:
Why didn't we all go this weekend?

"It's been a minute since I was on the ice," she said when we got there. "Let's see how much I remember."

Momma and Dad were all in, though they had never gone before. They laced up their skates, and Nana and I gave them some tips. They crept along the edge just like I did when I was learning. It was weird not seeing them as queen and king of the rink. Nana and I skated together and glided back to them to help.

It was a good day. On the way out, I saw a sign for hockey lessons. It was like it was lit up with Christmas lights. My eyes grew big. It made me think about what could be.

"What is it, Miles?" Momma asked.
Dad walked over and checked out
the sign. He smiled.

"For Willie O'Ree?" he asked.

"For Mr. O'Ree and for me."

I knew hockey would be another adventure, but I was ready. I gazed from face to face at Nana, Momma, and Dad. Something warmed me up from the inside.

I had all I needed to succeed.

Miles's Five Facts

My dad teaches Black history. He's all about learning as much as you can. I guess it rubbed off on me. I collect info about important people and events.

Here are five facts about Willie O'Ree:

1. Willie O'Ree grew up in Canada. He was legally blind in one eye. When joining the Boston Bruins, he kept it a secret, so he could play on the team.

2. He became the first Black player in the National Hockey League on January 18, 1958.

3. His Jersey number, 22, was retired by the Boston Bruins to honor him for being a trailblazer.

4. When he was a teen, Willie O'Ree watched Jackie Robinson play and met him. As a grown-up, he met him again. Can you believe that Jackie Robinson remembered him?

5. He was inducted into the Hockey Hall of Fame in the category for people who helped build the game.

Acknowledgments

I'm thrilled to have a new chapter book series. If you've read my stories about Jada Jones, you know her buddy Miles appears in most of them. I had no idea that one day I'd be writing books with him as the star. Thank you for joining me on his first adventure.

I see Miles in my children and in kids at every school I visit. They're smart, kind, funny, and sensitive. It's that last part that sometimes gets overlooked. Miles, like so many of you, feels deeply. He cares about his friends and family. He pushes himself to do well. He makes mistakes and discovers new things about himself along the way. These books are my tribute. I see you and want the world to see you, too. You're special, unique, and amazing. You shine just by being who you are.

So get ready for more Miles. Science, sports,

gaming, family, friendship, and community—he'll explore all that and more. Creating this series has been a blessing, as is the team who made it possible. I'm so grateful to have the best one around.

Thank you always to my brilliant editor Renee, the rock stars at Penguin Workshop, gifted illustrator Wayne Spencer, and my loving agent, Caryn Wiseman. Family and friends mean everything to me. Thank you to them for celebrating this project and every new book I write. Special shout-outs to my mom, brother Kevin, Aunt Dee, sister-friends Judy Allen Dodson and Susan Taylor, and sorors Shelia Reich and Dr. Pauletta Brown Bracy for their support and feedback on this book.

And now, here's a
sneak peek at the next

MILES★LEWIS
WHIZ KID

You know it's science fair time
when you see posters in the
hallway showing kids with
cool projects and people looking
amazed. Erupting volcanoes. Soda
bottle tornadoes. Bouncy eggs. As
I checked out the pictures, a grin
stretched across my face.

Soon I wasn't in the hallway of
Brookside Elementary anymore.

I could see myself onstage saying thank you as someone handed me a golden medal. Usually, I didn't care about winning. But this was different. This was my do-over. I had to get it right.

Last year, I created a switch that controlled the flow of electricity and turned a lightbulb on and off. I couldn't wait to set it up and let my friends try it out. Everybody said I was gonna get one of the spots to represent our school in the regional competition.

But as I walked around, I saw other projects that put mine to shame. I cheered for the winners, but walked away knowing I could have done better. I promised myself I would try harder this year. I was a future scientist—time to show it.

"What's up, Miles?" my best friend RJ said. I almost forgot he was standing next to me. "You're staring at that poster like it's a puzzle you got to figure out. You coming to class?"

"Yeah," I said. "Just thinking about the science fair. I'm going to be ready."

We entered Miss Taylor's sunny classroom and tucked our backpacks in our cubbies. My friend Jada was putting hers away, too. Jada and I were in science club together. I knew she would be as psyched as I was about the fair.

"You know what time it is?" I asked.

"Yep," she said, her braids and beads bouncing as she nodded. "Science fair. I want to do something really special. I'm getting started on my project as soon as I get home."

"I know you'll come up with something great."

"You will, too," Jada replied. "Got any ideas?"

"Not yet."

As we headed to our seats, I wondered what I might do. It had to be something interesting and creative that would wow the judges. What science question could I ask and investigate?

After the announcements, Miss Taylor hit the chime that called us to the orange-and-blue rug for our morning meeting.

Chirr.

"Who saw something different on the walls when you came into school this morning?"

Lena's hand shot up.

"Science fair posters."

Smiles and cheers mixed with a few frowns and groans.